First published in the UK
2021 by Owlet Press
www.owletpress.com
Printed in China

ISBN: 978-1-913339-11-1
Text copyright – Samuel Langley-Swain 2021
Illustrations copyright – Katie Cottle 2021

STORM IN A JAR

SAMUEL LANGLEY — SWAIN

KATIE COTTLE

Arlo visited Nana every Sunday.

Her house was always full
of flowers, and she would
always have new sweets for
him inside a glass jar.

But one Sunday, Arlo's visit was very different.
Mum explained that Nana had 'passed away',
which meant they wouldn't see her again.

All the flowers had dried out and the sweet jar was empty.
As Arlo saw his family sorting everything into boxes,
he realised that Nana wasn't coming back.

"Wait," shouted Arlo as his uncle tossed the sweet jar into the 'charity shop' box. He grabbed the jar and held it tightly. The sugar inside flew up to form dusty little clouds trying to escape.

The next day, Arlo decided he would always keep the jar next to him.

It made him feel safe during the sad times.

Even though the clouds grew dull and grey, Arlo wanted to keep the smell of Nana and her house inside the jar. So, he never opened it.

Weeks passed. Arlo often felt sad as he thought of all the questions he wished he'd asked Nana when she was alive.

His sadness . . . turned to anger.

The jar felt heavy and filled with a moody sea swirling underneath the gloomy grey clouds.

At school, Arlo got into fights with the other children, who teased him for carrying the jar.

When the teacher spoke to him about it, Arlo clenched his fists. His body felt tense as he stared into the jar.

The clouds were getting

BIGGER and

DARKER.

Then,
LIGHTNING
began to
FLICKER.

As Mum gave Arlo a hug after school, the jar felt even heavier.

WAVES
WHOOSHED
WILDLY
inside the glass.

BROKEN BOATS and
GIANT, BLACK JELLYFISH
appeared, whirling around in the dark water.

That night, Arlo lay in bed trying to sleep.

As his feelings grew **STRONGER** and **STRONGER**,

the storm in the jar grew **ANGRIER** and **ANGRIER!**

"I'VE HAD ENOUGH!"

Arlo shouted.

He held the jar high above his head and . . .

. . . smashed it onto the ground.

The glass

SHATTERED.

LIGHTNING CRACKED.

THUNDER BELLOWED.

The storm escaped, shaking the whole house!

And the swirling sea took Arlo, his bed, the broken boats

and all of the black jellyfish

out of his bedroom window

and into the dark ocean beyond.

Then . . .

. . . the water calmed. Arlo was alone in his bed, sailing on a smooth, moonlit ocean. He saw something in the light of the moon . . . It was Nana, sailing away on a boat made of sweets and flowers.

She smiled at Arlo and blew him a big kiss.
Arlo waved back. At that moment, he knew that Nana
would be safe and happy, wherever she was headed.

The next morning, the jar was still there
with its sugary clouds swirling inside.
Arlo told Mum all about his scary, stormy dream.

She handed him the jar and whispered,
"Everything we keep bottled up inside
always finds a way of coming out."
With his hand in hers, they gently opened the lid.

The dusty clouds drifted from the jar
and floated out through the window.

Arlo let out a sigh of relief.
He could smell Nana, her house
full of flowers and the years of
sweets that had been in the jar.

"We all miss Nana,"
Mum smiled, softly.

That afternoon, Dad and Arlo took a walk
to the florist and the corner shop.

Arlo skipped home, holding a paper bag bursting with sweets.
The kinds that Nana used to buy for him.

They both sat on Arlo's bed.

"We won't be needing this anymore,"
Dad winked, throwing the lid into the bin.

After what had felt
like a very long time . . .
Arlo's face finally lit
up with a warm smile.

With a little water,
they placed Nana's favourite
flowers into the jar, one by one.

And they did the same thing together . . .

. . . every Sunday.

MAKE YOUR OWN STORM!

STORM IN A JAR SCIENCE EXPERIMENT

STORMY-BOTTLE CALMING CRAFT PROJECT

MATERIALS

Baby oil
Paint (you choose the colour)
A large sprinkle of glitter
Alka Seltzer tablet
A clear jar or container
Water

METHOD

Pour water into the jar until there's a finger's width at the bottom.

Add two tablespoons of paint to the water (but don't stir it).

Pour the oil on top until the jar's nearly full.

Sprinkle glitter into the jar.

Break the Alka Seltzer into pieces and drop them in, one by one to create your storm!

MATERIALS

A clean plastic bottle
A jug of warm water
60ml glitter glue
3 drops of food colouring
Around 80g mixed glitter

METHOD

Pour water into the bottle (about a third full).

Squeeze in the glitter glue and the food colouring and stir well.

Pour in all the glitter and give one last stir.

With the rest of the water, nearly fill the bottle.
Screw on the lid, tightly.
Shake, then RELAX!

Follow @owletpress on social media
or visit www.owletpress.com to learn more about us.

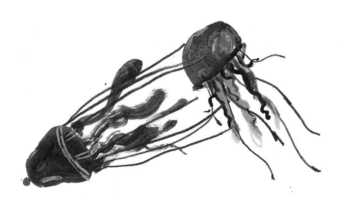

The
by th

Dylid
y dyddi

For Logan and his
great-great-nanny.
Love always. xxx